Erogenous
CONFESSIONS

By
Fauzykiss

Erogenous
CONFESSIONS

Fauzykiss
P.O. Box 19460
Detroit, MI. 48219

Email address: stephanie@fauzykiss.com

Website: www.fauzykiss.com
COPYRIGHT © 2006
By
Stephanie Fazekas

Cover Designed by: F.Alan Young (business@f-alan.com)
Final Cover Tanisha Bronaugh(tanisha@graphicinvite.com)
Photography: Marcus Parham (marcusparham@comcast.net)
Editing by Donna Lopez (exhortations.literay@yahoo.com)

First Printing August 2006

Printed and Published in the United States of America

ISBN 1-4276-0526-2

Erogenous
CONFESSIONS

Disclaimer

Dedication

This book is dedicated to my best friend, Ladonna Neal.
If writing erotic fiction is the only way I am going to share
my passion for reading with you...then here it is. I love you!

To my Grandmother, Mary Stokes, R. I. P.
To my Aunt Mary, R. I. P.

Acknowledgements

Above all I want to thank The Most High for walking with me always. Also I must take the time out to solute my ancestors—thank you.

To the best Mother in the world, Barbara. I want you to know that I appreciate your beauty inside and out. I am grateful that I have the ability to see your greatness while you're on this earth. You are unselfish, kind, loving and smart. It feels good to have you in my corner no matter what. You always make me smile on the inside when I'm crying on the outside with your wisdom and words of encouragement—I luv you!

To my child, Tory Jr., You are my biggest inspiration. Everything I do is for you. Keep smiling with your mouth and your big eyes—I love you better.

To my brother Tristin FazekASS, get it? I only say the things I say to you out of love and concern for my little brother. I want the best for you and yours. You have so many talents...use them; I wish I could do what you do with numbers in my head.

To my Father John thank you for always being here for us you never miss a beat. We are truly blessed to have you in our lives—I luv you too.

To my Godmother/Aunt Bridgette—you have always been a guiding light in my life. Thanks for being there when no one else was. I Love You. Kiss You Bye.

To my King Kwame, the sexiest, strongest, most intellectual and creative Black man I know. I know I am not the easiest woman to get along with sometimes and for this I want to thank you by loving me unconditionally through my moods and emotions. You keep me grounded when I am floating away—it's you and me Papi.

I am so grateful of my God Parents, Ace and Arlotta Bender. You two have touched my life in more ways than you know. I love you both.

To my Sister-in-Law, Eboni…no scratch that…to my Sister Eboni, you are very beautiful and intelligent and don't let anyone tell you otherwise. Remember nothing beats a failure but a try so get out there and PURSUE your dreams. I love you girl.

I also want to thank the following people for their love and support:

Brenda Bell, Lydia Loukas, Jaquita Howse, Sharice Nelson, Sonya, Sonja Dyer, Shari Drew, Amy, Vana Thomas, Gazel, Kelli Green, Wee Wee, Ken, Sysali Donald, Lawanda Mack, Enoch McFarland, Artegia Montgomery and Family, Mia, Dawn and Kareem Hamilton, Ava Wava, My Mother and Father in Law Tynetta and Michael Collins, Kambia, Uncle Bob Fazekas, Uncle Gary, Aunt Claudia, Uncle Sunny, Aunt Deborah, Uncle Leo, Ant Crystal, Uncle Sam, Aunt Renee, Aunt Brenda Jones, R. and L. Skelton, Samantha, Nisha, Renise and Carl Cunningham, Shania and Chris, Marie, Ladawn, Lydia Cochran, Daren Cochran, China, Lakeia Gunn, Kelly Usher, Carla Bradley and Family, Work Alem, Mwalimu M. Kamuyu, Felicia Coleman and Family,

Marquettes Harris, Teresa Dowell, J. Harvell, Audrey Davis, Wilson, Bianca, The Brown Family, Toni Jackson, Granny, The White Family, The Body Family, Dewayne Bender, Ralph and Shanika Bender, Carlos Proctor, The Charm Center Family Bonnie, Peggy, Mama Lena, Margreta, Davon, Laurie, Alisa, Lisa, Mr. Kirk and Scurve. Zeek, Ronni and Vincent, Latisha Washington, Samantha Hollins, Deborah Weddle, Ladawn Russell, Gwen, Phyllis, Tina, Tony Shelton, Toya, Patrice Boyd, Brandy, Brennon, Denise, Jovon, Millie, Miya Williamson, Mia Kemp, Leslie, Sharlyn, Jovon, Mrs. Latonya St. Clair, Jabar, Marcus, Raymond, Anthony, Sybil, Curly, V, Mama Streator, Mama Kehemba and Family, My Kiswahili Family Aasit, Albert, Cassidy, Cheryl, Chris, Lawrence, Kamari, Karen, Kendall, Rickki, Melissa, Sharita, and Vikki. Tamara, Net, Lanita, Lyn, Tucker, Diane, Gerald, Bianca, Shapontae, David Davis and Family, Kela T., Rhonda Smith, Tanisha B., The Snob Shoppe Family, Mario, Chevon, Robin, Sean, The Hopkins Family, Sydney, Wilfred Cochran, Richard Fazekas, All my teachers and instructors and mentors throughout my educational endeavors, Ms. Walker from Courville Elementary, Ms. Corbett from Hanstein, Mrs. Capen, Ms. M. Mills, Mrs. Spratt, Ms. Merkerson, Mrs. Holmes, Mr. Wilson, Ms. Peoples, Mrs. Bullock, Ms. Ward, Ms. Jones, Ms. G Livingston, Mrs. Rhodes, Ms. Thomas, Ms. Williams, Dr. T. Morton, Monique Patterson, and Professor Bullock. My Wayne County Family Dr. Pryor, Dr. Bridges, Dr. Blanding, M. Peak, Ollison, Lemons, Jackson, Jones, Robinson, K. England, Regina, Cha- Cha, Bush, McCarter, Smith, Hargrove, Ward, Jordan, Sgt. Crook, and The medical Staff. The Children in my life Tristin Jr., Kalah, Autumn, Allante, Ellery, Ty'iana, Josh, Erica, India, Robert and Jesse,

Stephen and Kennedi Thomas, and Little Lester, Ryan and Evan. I would also like to thank everyone at Truth Book Store, Graphic Invite, and Spectacles Clothing, The Shrine of the Black Madonna and My Sisters and Me Restaurant.

I must also thank everyone who purchased Erogenous Confessions. THANK YOU.

If I left anyone out it was unintentional. I ask that you charge it to my head and not to my heart. Please know that I love all of my family and friends and I am thankful for every part (big or small) that every one of you have done to inspire, encourage, and/or assist me in my endeavors.

Fauzykiss

TABLE OF CONTENTS

Prologue

It seemed that Simone Cox had been in college for her entire life. The only thing that stood in between Simone and her Doctorate in psychology was the final stage of her dissertation.

"Calm down Simone, you're just having anxiety about going before the PhD approval board tomorrow."

"I know Mom, I can't help it. I am worried that the board won't approve my dissertation presentation."

"Why honey? You are the best sex therapist in the state, and I am sure what ever your project is it will pass with flying colors. Simone, tell me what your project is?"

"Mom because of confidentiality laws I can only tell you that I have asked my patients to keep a daily confessional journal. The purpose of the confessional is to give my patients a therapeutic outlet to thoughts or events that they cannot share with anyone due to the fear of rejection and judgment. With the permission of my patients I have taken an entry from each one of their journals and created a book that will contribute to the continuous study on sex therapy in the world of psychology. Mom, that's not all. I have my own confession."

"What is it child?"

A bit embarrassed to admit the truth to her mom Simone twirls the phone cord as she contemplates if she should divulge her secret to her mother.

"Well, you know I have been very busy with school and that I have not had the time to indulge in any relationship of my own, and well I...I mean I get aroused sometimes when I read my patients' confessions. Mom I have been living my sex life vicariously through my patients' sex lives. I will be happy when this is over so I can have a life of my own." Simone sighs.

"I was beginning to wonder about ya myself. Simone, you never bring a date to family gatherings, I haven't heard you talk about a man in over a year. To tell you the truth I was starting to think that you might be interested in women and trying to hide it from me."

"Ma, you are so silly, no I love men, just don't have time for one."

"Ok Baby, get some rest you have a long day tomorrow. I love you Dr. Simone Cox"

Simone laughs. "I love you too Mom. Goodnight."

Simone arrived at her appointment a whole hour early hoping to suppress her nervous energy. When it was time for Simone to present her project she was calm and confident. The expression on the faces of the dissertation approval board assured Simone along as she read each arousing journal entry to them...

Michigan Auto Auction

07-10-03

Dear Confessional:

I was standing in line at the Michigan Auto Auction concession stand, as I have done every other Saturday for the past two years, when this gentleman tapped me on the shoulder notifying me that my money was hanging out of my pocket. The man had the warmest eyes I have ever seen. His skin was my favorite color, sepia. His stature would make any woman feel safe. He was thick in all the right places and the bass in his voice vibrated throughout my body. *Damn I wouldn't mind fucking him.* I thought to myself. So many wild and risqué thoughts ran through my mind as he commented on the gaudy five carat ring that dressed my wedding finger.

This was Damon's way of, "playa hatin", thinking the ring would keep men away. The ring was more like a promise ring, Damon did not have any intentions of getting married

within the next six years and I dammed sure
didn't. His motives never worked in his favor.
The ring actually attracted men to me. I
thanked the gentleman and placed my order.
After receiving my food I left to find Damon so
I could give him his chips and pop. I needed to
get to the ladies room in a hurry.

My panties were moist just from the site of
the gentleman. I have never met a man who
made me feel like I wanted to do him on the
spot until this hot summer evening. Maybe
tonight was going to be a full moon. Or maybe
it was due to the fact that I was sexually
inhibited with Damon; our lovemaking had
limits that he imposed.

I had to repress my sexual desires with him
and I must admit it has taken a toll on our
relationship. "Repetitive" is the best word to
describe our intimate relationship. We
performed the same routine all the time and if I
tried to be spontaneous Damon would
somehow make everything regular eggular. I
had resulted to self-pleasure, watching porno
flicks and purchasing nude male magazines. I
fantasized about Damon as I pleased myself
with one of the many of my dildos, but all of

this is becoming mundane and unsatisfying. Talking to Damon about our sex life upsets him and always escalates into a big quarrel.

I am a young woman who is very much in touch with her sexual side. I don't know how much longer I can fight the temptation of straying to another man to give me sexual healing.

I was leaving the ladies room, when I ran into none other than the very gentleman, who had me in this state. I observed that he had a fan club with him. He inconspicuously blew me a kiss nearly sending me back into the ladies room. *Get yourself together girl,* I told myself as I walked towards my man. Damon noticed my chipper mood and assumed it was because I saw a vehicle I wanted to purchase for our car lot. He left me to take a look at the motorcycles and four-wheelers on the very far side of the building.

When I felt someone blowing in my ear I thought, *maybe my baby is changing for the better.* As I elatedly turned to greet Damon with a kiss, I was shocked to see the gentleman. He stepped back, not sure of how I was going to react, and motioned for me to follow him behind the auction booth. Inquisitively, I ensued. He immediately asked me if the man he just saw leave my side was my husband. I guess I gave him the answer he wanted to hear. Mr. Gentleman stuck his tongue so far down my throat I could swear it touched my lungs. I enjoyed every bit of the kiss but I did not want Damon to walk up and witness this so I pulled back. I told the gentleman to meet me in five minutes. After telling him where to find me I looked around to see if I could see Damon. The coast was clear and I made my move.

I knew that Damon never looked for me when we went to the auction, I always found him. I got to my F-250 heavy-duty pickup before the gentleman, but he was not far behind. When the gentleman arrived we did not waste any time, I let out the emergency air mattress in the cab of my truck and we went to town. I never knew that money had any use other than making purchases—until the gentleman tickled every inch of my body with a brand new fifty-dollar bill. Each and every crease and crevice on my body smiled with delight. I don't know how the gentleman knew that my inner thighs were the key to my pussy.

His lips felt sooo good on my thighs. As he lightly kissed them I damn near climaxed. Before I could, he groped my thirty-eight double Ds, flicking his tongue around my nipples like a fan on high speed. The gentleman did not miss a spot giving each breast the same amount of attention.

Wanting to please me some more with his mouth, the gentleman asked me to sit on his face, I did him one better. I got on top of his six-pack in the sixty-nine position. I tickled his scrotum while I tenderly licked the head of his dick. His begging for me not to stop and his moaning only motivated me. After getting all nine inches of his manhood wet with slow, passionate tongue strokes I happily received him in my mouth, not releasing him until he climaxed. Although the oral copulation I received made my body quiver, I did not allow myself to cum. I'd rather wait until he was inside my magic box. Still rock hard, the gentleman laid me on my back spreading my legs to distances I did not know they could reach. After four slow, intense strokes I exploded. I tried to contain my screams of pleasure by biting my arm, leaving a not so pretty bruise.

The gentleman requested to see my bowling balls so I got on top. I do not know what his sextant touched but I experienced my first vaginal orgasm ever. My sweet juices flowed out of me like a broken dam. This did not stop the gentleman from getting behind me riding my ass until we came together. I was in HEAVEN! I had climaxed three times already and still wanted more. I usually did not want my clit to be touched after cumming twice. If any one ever called this gentleman a two-minute brotha they were lying to themselves.

Just when I thought all had come to an end the gentleman traveled down south wetting my mandinga up while stoking his mandingo awake so he could give me more. Getting back on top, the gentleman gyrated hard and fast. I moved in sync with his rhythm sending both of us into pure divine ecstasy. Wiping me first and then himself, the gentleman thanked me and left.

The pleasure was all mine. After putting everything back in place and checking to see if things were normal I returned to the auction. I found Damon purchasing one of several cars. He noticed my arm and asked what happened I told him I had been bitten by a kind of bug that I had never seen before.

It puzzled Damon that I did not advance on him sexually in bed that night as I usually did. He asked me if I was sick. I told him I was fine, I just had big things on my mind. Truth be told, I was floating on clouds nine, ten, eleven, and twelve. I was still mesmerized from my amour earlier that day. I never imagined that I would partake in something so risky, yet gratifying. I will hold on to the memory forever. I'd have to. We did not exchange any personal information. I probably will never see the gentleman again...except in my dreams.

Rainbow Roundtable

07-02-04

Dear Confessional:

Once again the Rainbow Roundtable and I have experienced what it feels like to be sexually liberated. Sunday we went to The Blend to celebrate our fellow member, Brittany's, birthday. Believe you me; it was a night neither she nor any of us will ever forget. The name of our clique described us in a very large nutshell. Our close-knit group consisted of eleven beautiful, yet intelligent and independent divas. We all have prominent jobs and are in the prime of our careers. Our beauty as a group left a little to be desired. Each of us represented a different shade of the black race from vanilla to blueberry, hence the name Rainbow. Our various physiques displayed that real women have curves. Those among us had petite asses, big asses, large tatas, small perky tatas (that screamed to be sucked), thick thighs, small waists—you name it our crew had it.

We walked to our VIP table, which was centered in the middle of all the action, allowing us to view everything that went on from various angles. Club Blend was always lit with all kinds of excitement due to its diverse crowd. The club was full of visiting celebrity athletes and entertainers. You could also find heterosexuals, homosexuals, the haves and have-nots, couples and single people partying it up at The Blend. I must add that the DJ was always on point, which, by my standards, was rare in Detroit. Not only did he play a wide variety of music, (old school, new school rap, R&B, and Jamaican slow grind music) he was, in my opinion, the main attraction of the club. He is very sexy. Physically, he defines all that I desire in a man. Umm, he is tall, chocolate, and muscular. The bass in his voice made my pussy vibrate every time he spoke.

Breaking myself from the trance I was under, I left the table to find a waiter or waitress so the girls and I could get blown away. Coming back with a waiter in tow I arrived just in time to witness this guy combust all over himself as

Brittney finished giving him her infamous hand job. Very turned on by what I saw, I smiled at Brittney and wished her a happy birthday. Everyone ordered their drinks and talked shit, as normal.

It was time to get the festivities of the night started. I proceeded to the DJ booth, which was more like a room. You could not see the DJ from outside the booth and had to ring a bell to get his attention. When he answered the door I asked him to give a birthday shout out to Brittney.

Licking his full lips he asked, "What are you going to do for me?"

I puckered my lips and asked, "What do you want me to do my African King?"

"Uh...be creative", he replied.

He did not say anything but a word and it was on.

After stripping down to my birthday suit I looked out the one-way mirror at the crowd as he put on a CD that was going to work for him while he worked on me. Sneaking behind me, I was amazed by his very hard dick that pressed up against my ass. Shit. For the first time I was not sure if I could handle such a long and thick dick, but like my mom always told me; nothing beats a failure but a try. I slowly turned around and was met with passionate kisses from my lips to my toes. When DJ returned to my lips, I observed his well-defined six-pack and aggressively unbuckled his pants, exposing his manhood. I was definitely in for a treat or two.

DJ picked all of my 38-24-36 self up placing me on his shoulders so that my pussy and his face collided. His tongue felt like a massive instrument in my pussy. It was extensive and erect. I came twice before he put me down. He immediately tried to fuck me but I interrupted him. I had been imagining what he smelled and tasted like for the last two years. I was not about to let the opportunity pass me by. I pushed him against the wall and got on my knees. I started first by licking his balls one by one then placing them in my mouth, in an in and out motion, all the while caressing his dick. His moaning, along with the way he pulled my hair, turned me on and made me want his dick in my mouth fast and in a hurry. I sucked his dick strong with no hands, for a few minutes— maybe five, before he let go in my mouth. He tasted just as good as he looked—dark chocolate—my favorite. I got full off of his chocolate deliciousness.

Since DJ was still erect, I seductively asked him if he was ready for the entrée. He replied by sticking his long thick fingers in my pussy taking them out licking them one by one. Gently placing me on his lap I rode him in this huge Lazy Boy Chair. Might I add there was nothing lazy or selfish about the way DJ fucked me. In the back of my mind I knew that our escapade could not last long. After all he was on the clock and I had to get back to my girls before they got suspicious. We climaxed after several long strokes. We exchanged phone numbers and he gave Brittany her birthday shout out as requested.

Before I headed back to the crew I went to the ladies room to freshen up. I opened the door to the first stall and that's when I realized I was not the only one from the posse being naughty in The Blend that evening. My sister Kenya was busted, literally, with her man's thang in her ass, of all places. Better her than me. I do not like, nor do I participate in anal sex however, I do not mind watching the act.

A little aroused by what I saw I closed the door getting back to what I came into the bathroom for.

After accomplishing my mission I joined the crew. Tizzy, the loud mouth of the bunch, eyed me and asked very obnoxiously why I was walking knocked-kneed. I just rolled my eyes and sipped my White Russian.

I was sequestered to dance by one of the regular hot boys. The dance floor was packed as always. We found a spot in the back. I faced the mirror watching myself as I put my arms behind my head and hip rolled to the Jamaican rhythms. I felt his manhood stiffen. I turned to face him and was caught off guard not expecting to see my best friend being finger-fucked by her woman on the dance floor, I had seen and felt it all, in one night.

Head Hunter

06-25-05

Yo, Confessional:

I have been home from my 12-month tour of duty in Iraq, as a high-ranking Sharp Shooter, for two days now. The war and time away from home has made me appreciate the smaller things that life offers. Although I missed my parents, my siblings and friends, I missed getting my dick serviced most of all. I mean, with the aid of technology and international cell phones, I was able to communicate with my loved ones while over seas, but I could not release the tension in my scrotum with a warm female body. Making love to five fingers and lotion gets boring after the first couple go-rounds.

Now that I am home I'm looking for someone to "take it in the face", as (my favorite radio personality/comedian) Foolish says. I am on a mission. I have got to find a woman to deflate my balls. I put an ad in the "Searching for Pleasure Times" and it reads:

Black Stallion, average height, muscular, silky dreads, employed, no children, talented, multi-tasked, gargantuous sized pussy pleaser-tonsil teaser, great aim, and anxious to please. Seeking a Black WOMAN any complexion or height will do, short hair or long hair it doesn't matter as long as it isn't flammable, preferably someone employed, at least intellectual, little asses need not apply, small breasts with big nipples welcome. Most importantly: MUST GIVE HEAD—NO TEETH PLEASE! If interested, email pictures, (head and body shot), self-description and a recently received certified and sealed doctor's clearance to my web page: HeadSharpShooter@Enter.Cum Please, Serious inquiries only!

The responses I got were enormous. I had to create a second web page to accommodate all of the pictures and statements I received from prospective huntees. It took me three days to select the final candidates. I set up two dates a night for each day of the week. Fourteen women later I narrowed my selection down to three pretty ladies. Cindal appeared to be the most qualified. Her physical and mental attributes aroused my curiosity the most. She had the perfect sized lips for gripping a dick, and by the way she sucked on her fudge pop for dessert I would say she could suck dick without her pearly whites getting in the way. The two runner-ups Kendra and Smoke had great personalities, but their packages were not complete. I could not tell how their head service was by their actions so the only way for me to find out was to do the damned thing; give them the knob so they could slob.

In order to compare the ladies effectively I had to have the three of them at the same time. Following dinner and the club the after party was at the Hilton Garden Hotel. I set the rules and questioned them to see if the ladies had any concerns. They had none and the games were on. Each one of them gave me a run for my money but the winner just happened to be Kendra. Man I never thought a pair of lips could make cum shoot out of my dick—projectile. Kendra made me a believer. Good thing she was the last one to suck my tonsil pleaser because unlike Cindal and Smoke, Kendra made me nut in less than five minutes—with no hands.

On her knees, she sucked both my balls and licked my dick at the same time while playing with her pussy. Cindal and Smoke watched in amazement as Kendra acted as a suction cup on my dick.

Kendra is a keeper 'fo sho'. I found what I was looking for and then some in her and I am officially off of head hunting duty.

Twice as Nice

02-2-02

Dear Confessional:

I do not know what has cum in me...I mean over me. Yesterday I met with my fellow Law school classmate, Ronsheem, at his home to study for our up and coming bar exam. Studying at Ronsheem's was very relaxing and peaceful; in fact studying did not seem as tedious as I anticipated. Ronsheem shared his four-bedroom home with his identical twin Ronkeab. Usually Ronsheem and I studied at my apartment or the University Library so I never had the pleasure of meeting his brother. Ronkeab interrupted our study session just as Ronsheem and I were ready to take a short break.

Seeing the twins together, side-by-side, made my pussy pulsate and my insides quiver. I was transfixed by their ebony complexion so clear and shiny that I could see my own image in their skin. Being in the company of not one, but two, very intellectual, statuesque, broad chest, and bowlegged Black men ignited my hormones with such intensity that for the first time I climaxed with no physical stimulation. I needed to get myself together so I excused myself, fleeing to the restroom. After sitting long enough to gather my thoughts and comprehend what I just experienced I absolved my mind as well as my pussy. I joined the twins once more, this time with more restraint.

We discussed their plans to open a community facility that would consist of educational and recreational programs. I enthusiastically expressed my desire to start a woman's support group that would address women's issues and provide resources necessary to empower them. We shared our ideas and decided to meet again so that we could collaborate. Keeping on schedule, Ronkeab left Ronsheem and me to our studies.

Still a tad bit nervous from my secret episode earlier, I clumsily knocked over a jar of pencils. I immediately got down on the floor to retrieve the pencils. I was getting off the floor when I bumped my head on something long and hard. Ronsheem's dick and my face met for the first time. Dropping the pencils once again, I moistened his dick with deep slow hard mouth strokes. I think I enjoyed giving Ronsheem head more the he did receiving it. I was so into it, I almost did not notice as Ronkeab came into the room hiking my dress over my apple bottom, moving my thong over to the side, and sticking his firm tongue in and out of my ass. I screamed to myself that this was not happening to me. I could not actually be intimate with two men at the same time.

"Yesss! Yesss! Yesss!" I moaned as Ronkeab made my knees shake. His tongue fully provoked a clitoral orgasm that exploded in his mouth. I must admit being celibate for almost two years has turned me into a slut (for lack of a better word). However, what I was feeling was indisputable. Just as I climaxed Ronsheem joined me, panting as he ejaculated. I could taste him all over my lips. Since Ronsheem and I both had the pleasure of cumming it was only fair that Ronkeab share in the pleasure. I put the magnum gold on Ronkeab's dick with my mouth. Then I got on all fours with my ass perched in the air. Ronkeab spread my ass cheeks apart, saliva poured from his mouth into the crease of my ass. His warm saliva wet my pussy. His dick inside my walls felt even better than his head. He fucked me with long slow strokes as he played with my clit assuring that I received as much pleasure as he did. I had already climaxed twice and any doubts that I would not cum a third time were laid to rest when my clit got rock hard while I watched Ronsheem jack his dick looking at his brother fucking me. To signify to Ronsheem that I saw him, and intensify my orgasm, I placed my own breast in my mouth and flicked my tongue on my nipples. Before I knew it Ronkeab too had climaxed and was ready to let his brother take his turn inside my love nest. I was all in until someone began violently shaking me and yelling my name.

Who the hell is interrupting my mini orgy? I turned to see who could be so inconsiderate when I realized I had been out for the count. The twins explained to me that I hit my head on the table pretty hard when I was getting up from picking up the pencils. I had been unconscious for a half hour or so. I was disappointed and relieved at the same time.

All of the pleasure I had experienced was only a very vivid and pleasant dream.

Pleasure Principle

05-31-05

Dear Confessional:

How do you tell your husband, the man with whom you pledged vows, that he is not freaky enough in bed? The song by Ludicris tortured me all day: "Lady in the streets but a freak in the bed." That's me. Apparently, not all men desire a freaky woman. At least not mine. Don't get me wrong our sex life is not awful, but it could definitely use some spicing. Qulil is usually content with the same boring positions. Me on my back or me on top. The latter being his favorite probably because it is less work for him. Not only does he get the pleasure of viewing my breasts while I ride him but he knows, without a doubt, that he will climax sooner in this position.

My dilemma is that I do not know how to tell him to talk nasty to me, slap me on my ass, push me up against the wall, be aggressive. It's obvious that I require diversity in the bedroom. Qulil is so missionary that he does not want me to give him head. Now this is getting out of control.

He knows that I have a great need for oral gratification. Yes, that's right. I have an oral fetish. I looooove sucking dick. The opportunity for me to please my man and myself with my lips rarely presents itself. Of course I have expressed my desire to Qulil but he does not take me seriously or want me to give him head. He insists that a woman sucking dick is un-lady like. In fact, our latest argument was about a proposition that one would think any man would agree to. Since he felt like I would be less of a lady for sucking his dick I asked him to let me watch another woman taste his manhood. Once again he dismissed my idea with no thought. I am left untreated and never totally satisfied. I love my husband and cheating is not an option but what is a girl to do?

Well one horny afternoon I decided that I was going to put an end to my desires by satisfying them. I made an appointment to see a psychologist. Being a new patient I wanted to make a good first impression. I journeyed to the mall and bought a Muslim head wrap. I went back home got dressed or should I say undressed? I left the house for my appointment in my purchase from the mall. After filling out the new patient forms I was called in to see Dr. Kufu.

Dr Kufu introduced himself and asked me where my husband was. This was supposed to be a couples' session. I did not speak nor did I sit down. Dr. Kufu's facial expression showed that he was puzzled by my need to remain standing. He just began to read my reasons for seeking psychological help. When he finished reading my profile he asked me how I thought he could assist me in resolving my marital issues. I answered him by turning and locking his office door. Dr. Kufu immediately picked up his phone for security. I stopped him by hushing him with my finger and then sticking it in my mouth licking it like it was a Charm Blow Pop. With my free hand I opened my coat and allowed it drop to the floor. Now I exposed my knee-high stiletto boots and freshly groomed pussy.

"Lady, are you CRAZY? I am not into sex therapy, please put your clothes...I mean coat...back on and leave."

I was laughing so hard on the inside I could barely contain it. Before Dr. Kufu could have a heart attack I seductively removed my headpiece. When Dr. Kufu realized that I was Mrs. Kufu his mouth dropped to the floor in relief and shock. Before he could protest I was under his desk on my knees removing his foot-long from his slacks. I stroked his dick with my hand while I took each of his balls into my mouth juggling them with my tongue. Qulil's receptiveness turned me on more as I began sucking his dick, flicking my tongue across his head.

I achieved my goal. Qulil melted in my mouth and not in my pussy or my hand for once. My tunnel of love craved for my husband to explore it so I got on his desk welcoming him with open legs. I caressed my clit with my left hand all the while guiding his face to my pussy with my right hand. Damn! My man was almost as good as his wife at giving head. He knows precisely how to hold my clit with his teeth while at the same time flicking his tongue on it making my knees shake violently. Before I could climax all over his beautiful face, he stood me up and kissed me passionately. He then turned me around with my ass facing his dick, placing it in and out of my pussy with long hard strokes. The build up was unbelievable and before long our fluids mixed sending both of us to heaven.

Qulil fucked me so good this day that I knew that this was only a sample of things to cum. For now…I am more than satisfied.

Professor X

10-12-05

(*My first semester of college*)

Dear Confessional:

He is bald,
coffee complexioned,
very tall, about seven feet two.
His dick bulges through his jogging pants.
It appears to be nice and plump, too.

He is muscular.
I think he body builds in his spare time.
If my dreams came true he would be spanking my
hide.

He is intelligent and down to earth.
He certainly seems to recognize and appreciate a
woman's worth.

His teeth are white and pretty,
I would not mind if he put them on my titties.

His hands are long and large,
by the looks of them he is always the head brotha in
charge.

His feet are long and narrow.
With this Black Beauty in my presence how can I
keep my eye on the sparrow?

I spend hours in front of my dorm room mirror
making sure my appearance is the best.
I wear a push up bra and a blouse that exploits my
cleavage.

I always wear skirts for easy access and
Stilettos make me taller, just in case
I get the opportunity to kiss the ex-basketball baller.

I apply Victoria Secret's strawberry lip-gloss
because it is nice and thick.
It also accentuates my naturally full dick pleasing
lips.

I spray my favorite perfume, Christion Dior Addict,
hoping it will bring my English Professor closer.
English has never been a strong subject for me until
this semester.

I go to this class punctually and faithfully,
in fact I am always twenty minutes early.
Hey, the early bird gets the dick...oops...I mean the
worm.

Since I sit in the front of the class I have to make a
conscious effort not to sit with my legs spread open.
I fantasize about what it would be like to sleep with
Professor X.

With my Eager Beaver in my panties I make myself
climax as I sit in amazement with the professor,
I am not sure if any one has noticed it but I am the
teacher's pet.

I am anxious to help when he asks for volunteers.
When I leave class my panties are guaranteed to be
wet, Impregnated with pussy juice not sweat.

I have to find a way to get over my infatuation.
Maybe Professor will give me some during summer
vacation.

In the mean time and between time,
I just get off sitting in his class

Fantasizing about him grabbing my ass and kissing my neck,
Damn!
I get hot and bothered just thinking about sex with Professor X.

Instant Climax

03-23-04

Dear Confessional:

I was in my early twenties when I realized that there is nothing that a man can do for me that I cannot do for myself. I can pay my own bills, purchase my own car, and please myself sexually. I find masturbating to be very beneficial and less of a headache than getting it on with my human counterpart. The pros heavily outweigh the cons. When I please myself there is zero chance that I will get pregnant or contract a venereal disease. I open my legs at my convenience and I know just where and how to elicit an instant orgasm.

I must give praise to a friend of mine who invited me to her adult toy party. To my delight I was intrigued by the toys that were on the market. I purchased two hundred dollars worth of merchandise some for friends but mostly all for me.

Buried in my nightstand drawer my toys lay unopened and forgotten about. One evening I was trying to relieve a much-anticipated nut with this tall, light brite, almost white brother. The brother had it going on until he prematurely let loose before I could get mine. I was disgusted and was prepared to climax by any means necessary. I looked at brother and pushed his head down south but he would not budge. Shit! I was hot and ready when I remembered my toy drawer. Thinking back on the party in where I purchased my Bullet I was reminded of the high reviews the Bullet received. I pulled it out to see if it was as magical as the ladies claimed it to be.

Boy, I tell you; from that day to this one the Bullet has my nose wide open. Every time I get an urge to tingle down yonder I grab my Bullet and go to work like the Pistons' theme song. I make love to myself better than any man could dream of. To heighten my experience I light cherry lemonade scented candles, I spray my silk sheets with Jean Paul Gaultier Cologne. This scent turns me on. I put on my Floetry CD and pop my favorite adult film in the DVD player. Finally, I check to make sure my batteries are fully charged. I certainly don't want my Bullet to go out on me in the middle of my nut, like ole boy.

Before turning my handy dandy dick on low speed I rub a little KY Oil on it. Massaging my big thighs, I work my way up top to my luscious brown nipples because I like them erect. After arousing my breasts I like to run my Bullet up and down my torso on high speed. *Ooh, umm, it feels sooooo good when I'm in control.* I spread my legs wide, wide, as wide as they can go. I stick my man in and out of my moist pussy. I want to cum instantly but I hold off so that I can roll over on my stomach and ride my Bullet until my juices flow out and saturate my sheets.

Now that's an instant climax and I can have one any time, any place, and at my own discretion.

Male Escort

08-19-02

Dear Confessional:

I am a woman on the move. My job as an Ambassador-at-Large requires that I travel to various places at any given time. I am usually in a particular place for no longer than six months at a time. My profession is very rewarding intrinsically as well as extrinsically. How many people get paid to venture the world? I have had the pleasure of meeting all kinds of different, but beautiful people as well as viewing the different landscapes.

Because my job is demanding, my life outside of work is very limited. Convenience is a 'must have' in my world, which consists of convenient food, living, transportation, and companionship.

I have not had a steady relationship in the past five years. I tried the long distance thing but it just did not pan out for me. This is why, when I have to attend an event that requires a date, or I build up a great deal of stress, or I just need sexual healing, I get escort service referrals.

My latest assignment was in Amsterdam, the capital of the Netherlands. I had been working really hard with the government to get a bill passed, which occupied most of my time. I was in meetings sixteen hours a day.

When my mission was complete I was stressed and had a lot of pent up sexual energy. I had an honor awards ball to celebrate the passing of the bill. I needed a date for the evening and the boudoir. Since Amsterdam was the land of sexual freeness, opportunity, and understanding, I did not think that setting a pleasurable date was a problem.

My sister, who lived in the area, referred me to Sex-On-Us Escort Service. I called right away with little time to spare. I requested a black man with dreads, preferably tall with broad shoulders and big hands. Since they asked if I had any sexual preferences I requested that the escort sent must also perform oral sex and be excellent at it. Sex-On-Us assured me that I would be satisfied. They prided themselves on providing services to meet all preferences and needs, because they did not give refunds. Great! I thought I should have a memorable evening.

I was impressed when the stud arrived at my hotel suite fifteen minutes early to begin our evening together. The conversation on the way to the ball was intriguing. The escort was down to earth; we actually had a lot in common. The escort's jokes helped to relieve my tension.

When we entered the ball all eyes seemed glued on us. It seemed like everyone at the ball tried to make small talk with us just to look at us up close. My mind was on what the end of the evening would bring. I was anxious to see what the stud was like in the bed. What can I say? I was horny.

I waited patiently for recipients of the awards to receive their honors before my date and I snuck away to our own ball. I made myself behave in the back of the limo on the way to the hotel, despite my urge to rip the escort's clothes off his physique. After all I did not want to frighten him by making him think I was an animal in desperate need of being tamed.

When we reached the suite all was lost, the beast emerged full throttle. I let my dress drop to the floor exposing my breasts and bottom half but leaving my heels on. I pushed Mr. Stud onto the California king-sized bed. I was in a hurry, the anticipation was killing me softly, and so I helped the escort undress. His body was as beautiful as his face and personality. He was firm from his chest to his bulging calves. Just looking at him sent me to my own paradise. He was so fine I forgot that he was being paid to please me. I wanted to satisfy him so I placed his member in my mouth. Within a couple of minutes he was shaking and releasing his ding-dong cream. *My turn.* I was ready to be eaten like the Last Supper. To my disapointment the stud rolled on a rubber and fucked me, as if to say eating pussy was not in his vocabulary.

The stud could tell by sudden loss of speech and the stiffness in my body that I was not a happy camper. He asked me what was wrong and I told him. He apologized explaining that he did not perform oral favors. I accepted and apologized as well, telling the escort I could have sworn that I specified when placing my order that the date must give head.

I lost my appetite for any sexual activity. I paid the escort, thanked him, and sent him on his way. Sex-On-Us however, was not off the hook so easily. I called them right away demanding to speak to a manager. After waiting on hold for about twenty minutes the assistant manager came to the phone. I explained the situation and asked for a partial refund since the misunderstanding was the company's fault. My request was denied, but they offered a replacement escort. Like I said my appetite to be pleased had dissipated. A replacement that evening would not be acceptable. Because I was returning home to Detroit the following day, a rain check would not suffice either. The assistant manager would not budge and neither would I.

I emailed the president of the agency. I included the details of my experience with his company from beginning up to the email I was sending him. I described how slighted I felt that his company got off at my expense. I had been left with no release because one of his employees screwed up. Just to make sure I got a response I added that I would use my political position to make sure that Sex-On-Us receive some bad publicity.

I received a call from the agency's president so fast that it made my head spin. He agreed to give me a full refund and promised to have one of his employees hand deliver it to me first thing the next morning.

Unlike the first time, this time Sex-On-Us held true to their word. I awoke to soft taps on the door. I looked through the peephole and the most gorgeous African man I have ever seen stood outside my door. He was dressed in a very expensive suit, hinting to me that he was not room service. I opened the door to the man who said he was the president of Sex-On-Us. He said he was there to deliver Ms. Hargy, Ambassador-at-Large, a check.

When I reached for the check the president offered more than I expected. I was swept off my feet and placed on my bed where the president fondled my jewel until I relieved all my stress juices on his face.

The president left telling me that he built his company by 'word of mouth' it is his job to make sure all of his customers are completely satisfied, so that they would continue to patronize his company. Now that's what I call customer service at its best!

Vegas

12-28-04

Dear Confessional:

Last Friday, Melody, Aza and I were sitting around having our monthly ladies' night. We were drinking apple martinis and smoking joints, when out of nowhere my best friend, Melody's, name was echoed through her state of the art entertainment system. All of us studied the room in confusion. We couldn't figure out who was calling out for Melody, or how. We thought we were the only ones in the condo.

Finally, we realized that it was the Disc Jockey on the radio announcing that Melody was the winner of the 'trip-a-day giveaway'. We screamed and danced around a minute or so before she called the radio station to claim the prize.

Melody won one a trip for three to any location she chose within the United States. A month to the day we landed in Sin City. It was the first time any of us had been on the West Coast and we were all bubbly with excitement. On the shuttle ride to Caesar's the tour guide reminded us that what happens in Vegas stays in Vegas. I guess the saying that "rules are meant to broken" is true—cause I brought something back from Vegas—an itch to be precise. It's not the itch that bothers me so much. It's the fact that it can't be scratched. The guy who infected me is probably spreading his contagiousness to more unsuspecting women.

UGH! I wish he were here, I would smother his face with my everlasting wound, until I could no longer squat over him. Yes, I'll be the first to admit that in Vegas I got more than I bargained for. Normally, I was more conservative with my sexual activities. In fact I am still trying to figure out how I even got in this position.

I remember my friends dragging me from my poolside retreat to go to Club 7. So I hold Aza and Melody partially responsible for my aliment, even if it is just to make myself feel better. When we got to the club Aza and Melody abandoned me. They actually left me at the bar to fend for myself, while they went to shake some tail feathers. I am assuming that I appeared to be lonely because this white guy sat next to me when there were ten empty bar stools on both sides of me.

Initially, I was not interested in indulging in any type of communication with this stranger. After a couple of drinks I became friendlier and was more receptive to his small talk. We formally introduced ourselves and the more we talked the more attracted I became to the stranger also known as Kevin. I questioned my attraction for Kevin because I had never been attracted to white men before. Kevin's olive skin tone, dark, wavy tresses, thick eyebrows and long eye lashes aided in my attraction for him. I prefer men with dark features, it seems, but it was really Kevin's funny sense of humor that won me over.

The caged dancers must have sparked my libido because Kevin and I went from talking about his Sicilian roots to his hotel room. Once I crossed the threshold I knew there was no turning back. I agreed with myself to make the best of the evening. I didn't know what to expect. I'd heard all the myths about white men leaving a lot to be desired in the size department. I was hoping for the best, I wanted something to brag to my girls about—especially since they left me alone in that big, ole club.

When it came to being romantic Kevin excelled. Kevin wasted no time lighting candles throughout the suite before he ordered strawberries and champagne. Adding to the mood, he went as far as adding black cherry scented bubble bath to the Jacuzzi. He was really proving to be something different inside and out for me. I was not used to men taking the romantic approach. I was astounded.

Sensing my apprehensiveness, Kevin left the room so that I could get undressed. I slipped into the Jacuzzi, hiding my nakedness, until I felt more comfortable. After getting acclimated to the water my body went to another level. I closed my eyes and was taking in everything when I felt Kevin enter the Jacuzzi room. My eyes bucked when I saw his massive erection. Oh boy! Did he shatter the stereotypes—in a major way. I remember thinking, *how is he going to get his large bat and balls inside of my cage?*

I began to have second thoughts. It may be best if I go back to the club with Aza and Melody. Kevin, obviously used to this reaction, immediately began assuring me that he would be gentle, specifying that his manhood did not feel as long as it looked.

Kevin broke the ice by playfully splashing water, instigating a water fight that led to passionate kisses. Not wanting to rush the moment Kevin exposed me to a new kind of foreplay. I told Kevin about my love for books and reading and he used this to his advantage. Kevin read me an erotic story. I was flattered and ready to give him all my goodies. He, however, was not ready to give me something I could feel at that moment. Sitting across from one another in the water Kevin gazed into my starry eyes. He poured champagne on my toes, sucking them one at a time, sending sparks up my tailbone. The more he sucked the more my body slid down in the Jacuzzi until my black box collided with his magic wand. Subconsciously, I pushed myself back to my end of the tub. Before I knew it Kevin pulled me out of the water and began drying me off with his tongue. I was so caught up in the moment that I can't recall how I ended up on the bed with Kevin's tongue in my pussy. I do remember how good it felt when Kevin nibbled on my prawn of pleasure, making my knees tremble violently.

WHEW! I had not experienced that one before. It was at that point I knew why Aza and Melody were infatuated with having their southern kitchens eaten. Kevin tickled my clit 'til I couldn't take anymore. I tried to sit up and crawl away from Kevin, but he tenderly pushed me back, silently telling me he was in control. I liked aggressive men in bed. I submitted without a fight. I grabbed the sheets so I could take the tongue lashing like a woman.

By the time Kevin got done salivating in my black box I was gasping for air, searching for enough of it to tell him to stick his dick in me. After teasing me he stroked my kitten with his manhood until the sheets were drenched with our perspiration. Kevin never did cum. I asked him why and he said that he couldn't with the sheath on.

"Too bad... not in this lifetime. I was not going bareback no matter how good the lovin' felt. Call

me selfish, but I got mine, so I was not concerned at this point. Kevin did not seem upset. We took a shower together where he went down on me again, making juice run all down my legs.

Kevin took it upon himself to help me get dressed. He walked me back to the club. I found my girls waiting for me at the bar where they had left me earlier. They were worried because they didn't have a clue as to where I disappeared. After divulging my eventful evening they forgave me for scaring them.

The rest of our vacation was enjoyable but I couldn't wait to get home. I called Kevin, against my better judgment, in hopes that I could, at least, tell him what I thought about him.

After five days he still had not returned my call. Now I'm left to suffer through this itch as it spreads so far that I cannot scratch myself.

Wife Beater and Timbos

6-11-06

Dear Confessional:

His grey eyes caught my attention, but his Timberland Boots and wife beater t-shirt had my pussy boiling. I have a fetish for Wife Beaters and Timbos. When a beautiful rough neck brotha sports the attire I cannot control my hormones. I patted my crotch reminding her that we were at work and must be professional.

The County Jail was not the place to be meeting the man of my dreams. It was obvious from where he stood that he was visiting one of the many brothers on lockdown. Birds of a feather flock together I told her, but she had a mind of her own and she continued to pulsate against my queen-sized stockings.

I walked faster, hoping that if I could get this five foot ten specimen with caramel complexion, braided hair, long eyelashes, and succulent lips out of my sight, that he would be out of my mind and the fire under my skirt would smother itself.

I decided that it would be in my best interest to take the stairs to my office. If I were to wait for the elevator there was as a great chance that I would encounter the visitor. Besides I needed the workout. By the time I reached the fifteenth floor I was out of breath. I was heaving so hard that one of the officers offered to call a nurse. He thought I needed medical attention.

What I needed was sexual healing and more working out. My thighs, although toned, had become very heavy since I started working in the jail. For some reason I ate fast food more often than I did when I worked at the university and it has taken a toll on my body in just over a year.

When I reached my office I had several notes waiting for me. It appeared that a couple of inmates attempted suicide in the short hour I was away on lunch. I did not have time to sit and collect my thoughts, much less digest my food. I called for the files on the inmates. I wanted to review their histories so I would know how to best approach them.

After a thorough read I put on my lab coat and headed to the battleground. The first inmate was not serious about taking himself out. He more or less wanted attention. When the officers would not entertain him he cried suicide. I gave the young man some words of wisdom regarding what takes place on the suicide ward and his demeanor changed with the quickness.

The second guy however, actually wanted to die. He had been to court earlier that day, had been found guilty, and was facing natural life. Determined not to see prison walls, he created a noose for his demise. An officer on rounds found the inmate before he could succeed in taking his life.

Walking back to my office, passing the visiting booth, I spotted the same visitor speaking with an inmate. It turned out that he wasn't visiting a family member or friend. The booth they occupied was for professional visits only. The visitor had to be an attorney, a probation officer or a detective. I gambled on the latter due to his wardrobe. I could not see an attorney or probation officer wearing a white tee and jeans to visit a client. Either way this gave me more hope...I might be able to get to know the visitor better. At least I'd be able to daydream about what it would be like to feel him inside of me.

By the time I was through writing my recommendations for the inmates it was time to punch out. I was rushing to get home so I could take a nap and hopefully dream about the visitor.

I ran to catch the elevator. This time of day everyone fought for the elevators and I did not want to lose today. My exit was so hasty I almost walked right past the man I was going home to fantasize about. I was startled when I felt a huge but soft hand land on top of my shoulder. Turning to see who would dare touch me sent my mind and pussy into another battle. My attitude softened when I discovered the beautiful man in front of me. He must have sensed my concern and began to introduce himself right away.

Jason Hew was his name. Detective Jason Hew. He worked for the Detroit Police Department and was working on breaking a series of organized crime efforts within the department. After getting past the formalities we agreed to meet for dinner that evening.

Dinner was great but to my disappointment Jason did not make a move on me as we sat, drank wine, and listened to jazz. I enjoyed the date but did not like my panties being wet against my skin.

The next day proved to be more interesting than the day before. I was on my regular rounds checking on the inmates. I decided to take a shortcut to my office down a ward that was empty due to construction. Smiling on the inside, I hummed a tune out loud expressing gratitude for the pleasant evening I had the previous night. Suddenly I was pulled into a cell. Before I could think about screaming my mouth was covered by a strong, massive hand.

I was relieved when I saw Jason. He did not waste anytime before he slid his tongue in my mouth. As our tongues tangoed, most of our garments collided with the concrete floor. For my viewing pleasure I insisted that Jason keep his wife beater and Timbos on. I, on the other hand, was completely nude...with the exception of my six inch, Via Spiga, pumps.

I remember a sheath being on Jason's plunger but I don't know when he slipped it on. I do recall Jason lifting my leg placing my foot in between the bars and using my shoe as a wedge to hold my leg in the air. Jason entered me from behind grabbing my breasts as he moved in and out of my bottomless pit.

Remembering that I was at work in a jail I had to tone down my moans to below a whisper. This was hard. Jason's dick felt sooo, sooo gooood. I moved one of his hands down my stomach onto my clit where I motioned for him to massage her tenderly. When I felt like I was going to drip all over him before I wanted to, I pulled away from him. I turned to face him admiring how he fucked me in his large Timbos. We stood there and stared at one another for a brief second.

Then I turned around and bent over spreading my legs and touching my toes; signaling for Jason to enter me once more. Our rhythm seemed to be in sync instantly, as if we never stopped. The more I rolled my hips the tighter his grip around my waist became. We went on like this until my name was called on the PA system.

We went into a frenzy. But I was not leaving until I let out some cream and I have a feeling that Jason felt the same way. After emitting our double shots we agreed to get together later. Duty called once more and we went our separate ways...for the time being.

Driving While Black

08-06-05

Dear Confessional:

I am at odds with how I am going to tell my wife that I was suspended from my job without pay today. To make matters worse I think I may be in love with another woman that I could never have. You may be wondering why I got suspended. Well, it's simple and I do not have anyone to blame but myself.

Yesterday I was being the racist prick police officer that I was raised and trained to be. I was on traffic duty and I was trying to fulfill my quota for the month when I got lucky. A black 745-I BMW with a license plate that read: 'Driving While Black' had the nerve to pass me on the highway. I was livid. *Those people think they can do what they want. Maybe in the city, but not in my suburban neighborhood.*

Almost immediately after putting on my lights and sirens the Beamer pulled over into an isolated area. *Damn, today was going to be an easy day,* I laughed to myself.

With plans to write the driver as many citations as I could and hopefully give away a complimentary pair of silver bracelets. I approached the vehicle with arrogance. The windows were tinted so I had to wait until the driver lowered them to get a clear view inside.

The black beauty behind the wheel stunned me. Dr. Nyssa Jive, a renowned sexologist, greeted me. I secretly watched Nyssa's sex show when the wife would not entertain me, fantasizing on what it would be like to penetrate a black cock.

Attempting to stick to my plan I asked for license, registration, and proof of insurance. Nyssa handed me her info with no hesitation brushing her fingers against mine in the process. Nyssa's touch sent tingles down my spine and brought my dick to attention.

As I was examining Dr. Jive's information she questioned why she was pulled over. When I did not offer her a response she got quiet and began adjusting her blouse so that I could see her round hazelnut boobs. "Miss, I am going to have to ask you to step out of the vehicle while I go run your info through the computer."

"Sorry officer but I am going to refuse until you tell me what this is all about." Nyssa knew that she had not committed any traffic violations and was stopped because of her license plate.

"Miss you are cruising for trouble. Now do as I asked or you are going to force me to get hard with you."

"From the looks of your pants you are already hard."

Embarrassed by Nyssa's discovery I went to grab the door handle when she began to remove herself from the car. Standing face to face with the sex doctor made my heart race. No one could have paid me to believe that a black woman could make me feel this way. I had butterflies in my stomach. Nyssa turned me on in the worst way.

"Before I go to my squad car I must search you".

Turning around without a fuss Nyssa seemed to welcome my hands as I frisked her body. When I reached her hip area Nyssa hit me in the groin as she poked her ass out. My body shuddered. I could not control my erection or suppress my desire.

"Umm, Big Boy...your dick feels as big as it looks. I wonder how it would feel in my pussy."

That was it. I could no longer deny to myself that I wanted this woman. Just as I was going to let her leave she pulled my cock out of my pants and stroked it tenderly. *What would her wet pussy feel like, if her hand stroking my member felt so good? Could it get better?*

The sound of my radio snapped me back to reality. Now my radio and Nyssa competed for my attention. She nibbled on my ear and I ignored the radio.

"Breaker, Officer Ditz. What is your location? I repeat. What is your location?"

I turned the walkie-talkie off. I could not come out from under Nyssa's spell. My pants hanging around my ankles made it impossible for me to remain standing. I was seductively shoved onto her backseat. Somehow, she ended up lying face up. I mouthed her pretty pussy getting her juices to flow like a river in my mouth. I could not wait to stick my cock into her. She could tell I was anxious but she took her time rolling the rubber down my shaft. I was bending down ready to experience something exciting when colorful flashing lights blinded me.

My radio. I should have responded, now the whole damned squad has come looking for me. Before I could get my pants up I was surrounded by the Chief of Police and six other officers. They all got a good view of my rubber-coated dick.

"I see why you did not give your location, Ditz. You are knee deep in work." Chief Dana Jiski was sarcastic in her comment.

I tried to plead my case but my words fell on deaf ears. Nyssa explained to the Chief that she was pulled over for no reason other than her license plate. This is when I found out that Dr. Nyssa Jive was in town visiting her half sister, Chief Dana Jiski. Hmmph...sending me further up shit's creek.

Now I have to wait to find out if I will have a job or a future. I have to find a way to face my family, and my obsession with Nyssa.

Should Be Hard for a Pimp

June 2, 2003

Dear Confessional:

I have been backsliding for seven years now. I am not talking about recovering from substance abuse and going back either. I am talking about sliding on my ass performing sexual favors for money. I know that this is the oldest profession in the world but I am ready to call it quits.

Being a courtesan was not my dream occupation. I was forced into this lifestyle by my drug-addicted parents. My mother and my father bartered my body for drugs. When I was old enough to escape them I had no alternatives. I chose to sell my own body as a means to an end, so to speak.

I had no idea what a pimp was when I attempted to sell my goods independently. I managed to do fairly well until this "John" held me hostage in his moldy basement for two days. I managed to flee captivity screaming like a banshee until I passed out behind an abandoned building. When I awoke I was surrounded by a house full of gorgeous, well-kept women. After explaining to the women what happened to me, I discovered that I was recovering in the abode of the biggest pimp in the city.

The women insisted that if I was going to survive in the streets I needed the protection of a pimp. The whole pimp thing was embellished by the other women of the night and I; the naïve seventeen year, old fell for it. I was intrigued and I felt like I would have a family if I stayed. I chose Man as my pimp and the rest is history.

In the beginning Man was charismatic and kind. But lo and behold it did not take long for the other shoe to drop, right on my head. Man required 75% of my earnings and pussy on demand like a Comcast Cable show.

This went on for about a year. Being around some of my clients gave me some insight on life and a different way to view things. I began to consider leaving the stable and working for myself again. I was a little wiser but I still had to consider the dangers I faced in the streets without the protection of a pimp. Either way, I knew that I was not going to make it. Working for Man, I was getting my ass beat like it was a sport, and I was still barely making it financially.

It is time for a change. I am going to seek a new way of life. If it kills me so be it. If I continue to be a woman of the night I am going to die sooner than later anyway.

Drought

01-06-06

Dear Confessional:

   Longing for a man's touch is an understatement in an effort to describe what I am feeling right now. I have been celibate for a year now. This is a new behavior for me. The longest I have ever been without sex was two weeks. A venereal disease called Chlamydia is to blame for my abrupt drought.

   I was messing around with this guy named Cane. Our relationship was mostly sexual because he had a girlfriend and I was not trying to be committed. The dick was the bomb and the head was even better. Although, due to his relationship, I would not put my lips anywhere near his dick. I only know who I'm fucking and I do not play Russian Roulette with my health.

   One beautiful evening I invited Cane over for some drinks and pussy. After getting a little twisted we began to do what we do best together. Cane and I were in the middle of some hellified fucking when I noticed something different. I felt...or should I say...I didn't feel something. I pushed Cane off me in mid-stride, just before he could bust his nut. Examining his dick with scrutiny it was just what I thought. The brother had slipped the condom off. I knew when we began our sex session Cane had on a Trojan Magnum because I put it on him myself.

I could not believe him. I felt totally violated. There was nothing left for me to do but put Cane out of my apartment. I told him that I never wanted to see or hear from him again.

Cane knew that he blew it with me and did not pursue me any further after that night. One night about two months later Cane called me a million times. I sent his calls straight to voice mail every time...tired of calling me, Cane finally left a message. He urged me to go to the doctor because he and his girlfriend had been tested positive for the Claps.

What the fuck! I could not wait to go to the doctor so I rushed to the emergency room. All kind of thoughts ran through my mind as I drove to the hospital. I kept trying to assure myself that I was fine. I could not have anything because after the stunt Cane pulled I visited my OB/GYN doctor and all my tests came back negative. The situation made me apprehensive about being sexually active with anyone else.

Needless to say, after sitting in the emergency room for six hours my test came back positive for Chlamydia. How can this be? I asked the doctor. I was tested two months ago and everything was fine. The doctor told me that at that time it was too soon after contracting it for the disease to show up. *But I haven't had any symptoms...this must be a mistake!*

The doctor explained to me the disease often does not have any symptoms in women until it is too late. He told me that the disease had been living dormant in my body and that it was a good thing that I came in when I did or my reproductive organs could have been destroyed.

I left the hospital furious and trying hard to think of a plan to get back at Cane. By the time I made it home I came to my senses and decided to just leave well enough alone. After all, I was partly to blame.

Peeping Tonya

06-10-04

Dear Confessional:

The object of my affection is sooo long, ooohhh smooth and unbreakably hard. It allows for great satisfaction as I lean my body on it. The marble textured windowsill has been my favorite past time every since my husband died a year ago.

My husband was the first and only man I have ever been with intimately. My self-esteem is very low because I am obese. Derrick was the only person I ever felt comfortable enough with to allow a relationship to flourish. Since Derrick's death I have regressed to my reclusive behavior.

I have tried slimming down by trying every diet known to man with no luck. I have also made an effort to exercise but nothing seems to work. I have just accepted my two hundred fifty-nine pounds as my fate. At least I can enjoy the world vicariously through the people I view outside my window.

Most recently I've been inspired by my new next-door neighbors. The twin hunks, Caleb and Calvin, are not your average twins. The twenty-nine year old duos are conjoined at the hip. They have two pairs of legs, two pairs of arms, two heads, and most importantly for the sake of this letter, two dicks. I know this because I have been spying on their comings and goings through my long, hard windowsill.

I get excited every time I see them. I watch them with my binoculars, as they get undressed behind their bare window. Their six-pack stomachs turn me inside and out. When they take a shower I can't stop myself from perspiring, I can feel the steam all the way in my apartment. I shudder as they lather their bodies. All the while I picture myself washing their backs for them.

As I said before, I have been keeping an eye on their cummings and goings. It is apparent that I am not the only one with the hots for Siamese twins. Last night I observed the twins with the opposite sex for the first time. Home girl was a looker herself, with a shape to die for, flawless skin, and 'fuck me' pumps. The young woman came and did all the things I fantasized about doing to and with the duo.

I am not lying when I say that while in the 69 position the twins took turns searching for home girl's man in a boat, with their tongues of course, while she alternated the twins' dicks in her mouth. I thought that the oral orgy was something, but home girl proved that I hadn't seen anything yet. She performed multitasking skills they don't teach in business school. She was straddling Caleb's magic stick backwards while twisting her upper body so that she could lick the head of Calvin's magic stick. Amazing!

I thought they were going to bring the session to an end when I saw the twins lift forward grabbing girlfriend's tig ole bitties from behind, but I was wrong. They were just flipping home girl on her back taking turns going in and out of her hot box. When one combusted all over her belly the other received a hand job as he waited patiently for his turn to implode.

I could not hear what was going on but I am sure the audio was as damned good as the visual.

Cumsignment

12-11-03

Dear Confessional:

I had been to three adult novelty stores already and had five more to visit outside of the city. Up until today I had never been inside one of these stores. I was attempting to get the stores to put my adult novels on their shelves to sell on consignment.

This store was gigantic. Each section had to be at least one hundred square feet. I was amazed by the various items that were sold. I have never seen so many dicks and pussies in one place at the same time. Hell, pussy and dick don't come in cans but they sure do come in boxes. They even supplied pussy licking tongues and dick enlargers. What will they think of next?

I wonder if the penile enlarger machine really works.

I asked the fine store clerk, "Excuse me sir. Do these penis enlargers really work?"

Smiling, the clerk responded with pride, "Miss, I wouldn't know. I am large and in charge."

"That's what they all say," I said chuckling.

"I can show you better than I can tell you, lady."

"No, but thanks. I'm flattered, however, I spoke to the owner of the store yesterday about bringing my books in to sell."

"Oh, you are Fauzykiss! Yeah, Rick told me to expect you. Leave your books on the counter and I will sign your invoice. While I am getting your receipt together you can take a look around the store."

I did just that. I wanted to purchase an adult film to use as a muse, so I looked in the heterosexual section for one that might interest me. There were so many to choose from. I asked the clerk for his suggestion.

"Ms. Fauzykiss, I like them all. You might want to check out the peep show to make a more informed decision."

"Peep Show! I don't want to see people fucking live. That is a little out of my league."

He was holding his stomach laughing. "Lady you are funny. The peep show is not live. A peep show is a video you pay a quarter to preview before you purchase it."

My face turned several shades of red from my embarrassment. Here I am thirty years old, writing pornographic literature, and I do not know what a peep show is!

Since I always wondered what it looked like when two men fornicated I watched a short minute of guy-on-guy action. *Interesting*, I thought to myself. Curiosity did not kill the cat and it didn't satisfy her either. I immediately picked another booth to view relations that did not make me feel uncomfortable to watch. I found one with girl on guy action. I felt more relaxed.

I was happy with the second and third clips I viewed so I put them in my hand basket to purchase. The clerk was not done with my invoice yet so I browsed the store some more.

I discovered that there was something for everyone in the warehouse sized novelty store. There were real whips, chains, and handcuffs. There were magazines with my plus-sized sistas adorning the covers and naked couples doing the grownup. I picked one up and was in the middle of an article when the clerk called me over to the register. I purchased my porn's got my invoice along with a date to collect for my sales and left.

The peep shows brought forth urges I could not ignore. As for the sexy store associate, he and I grabbed a few items from the store and made our own peep show on his lunch break. The brotha wasn't lying when he said he was well endowed. His thang was so big I could not deep throat it if I wanted to. It sure felt good in my stomach though. I don't even need the tapes for inspiration anymore, I can write about my memorable escapade.

The next few stores were not as fascinating as the warehouse but I got all my books out of my house and onto someone's shelves.

Liquid Azz

03-17-06

Dear Confessional:

I know that after last night my grandmother is spinning in her grave because of my actions. It all began when I asked my fiancé, Ky'am, to go out with me and he declined.   He convincingly insisted that he had to meet with a very important client to finalize a business deal.   One monkey has never stopped any show for me. Unbeknownst to Ky'am I was going to one of the city's highly prestigious Gentlemen's Club, Liquid Azz. It was owned and operated by my older brother, Malik.

I normally do not frequent strip clubs however, this night, I was going to support my twin sister, Nidra. She had fallen on what you call hard times and would not accept help from her family or friends.

Nidra considered any financial assistance to be handouts and would not accept them. Nidra was very well educated and independent. She had obtained her Doctorate in Africana Studies and worked as the Director of Community Development for Ford Motor Company. Like many companies, Nidra's employer was affected by the slumping economy. She was one of many white-collar employees laid off by the downsizing of The Ford Motor Group. Nidra was accustomed to the life style and salary that Ford had afforded her. She depended on her earnings to fund the inner city organizations she founded in an effort to elevate the community.

She felt that it was imperative to sacrifice herself to help others so she returned to Liquid Azz as an exotic dancer. Nidra worked at Malik's club before to put herself through college. He never wanted his sister to work in the club. But she insisted and, as always, he gave in.

Our grandmother, like the parents of a lot of black families, did good to feed, clothe, and keep a roof over our heads. It was impossible for her to even think about putting away money for a secondary education. She wanted that for us but she wasn't able to help us at all. But we know that she would never want any of us involved with clubs involving exotic dancers.

Nidra was the main attraction at the Liquid Azz. Men from all over the world came to Liquid Azz just to see Nidra work her magic. Nidra made the club popular by bringing in millions of dollars annually by herself. Her earnings were lucrative and provided more than enough money for her to live comfortably even after paying an expensive tuition.

Nidra alone would cause my grandmother to spin in her grave. But, then, I went to Liquid Azz myself. I just sat in one of several balconies in the club, VIP of course, giving me a very good view of the club. I was in the middle of a very delectable dinner when I noticed Ky'am, and he was not alone. He was accompanied by a young woman who was supposed to be one of his clients. She was a very attractive client.

I found Ky'am's acquaintance quite interesting. She appeared to be more of a date (with her provocative, form-fitting shirt that exposed her large breasts, thigh high boots, and her very short, tight skirt). She looked as if she almost had on no clothes. It did not appear to me that Ky'am was closing a business deal like he told me earlier that evening, unless sealing his tongue down her throat was part of the business deal.

I was so out done I could not even get upset. I could not believe that Ky'am would be brave enough to take another woman to my brother's club and not expect to be seen. I had to get even. I had a couple of drinks to loosen up. I was getting ready to be devious now.

I went to my sister's dressing room to enlighten her on my discovery. Collectively we devised a plan that would allow me to get even with Ky'am. Instead of my sister appearing on stage I would take my adentical twin sister's place. I would appear as Sacha Devine, the exotic dancer.

The DJ introduced Sacha and the crowd welcomed her with loud cheers. I made my grand entrance to T-Payne's, "I'm In Love With A Stripper". Sacha seductively stalked the dance way like a panther hunting for her prey. All the while she was keeping a close eye on her fiancé and his new business venture.

Sacha did not make it on stage comfortably before she was sequestered by one of many men beckoning for her attention. She squatted down grinding her crouch in his face as he placed a very generous amount of money in her garter belt. She did the papoose pump for him and moved on down the stage.

Sacha was not sure how long she could play the exotic dancer because the G-string felt like a knife in her behind. Despite her discomfort she climbed the long, thick black pole gaining more attention than she expected. Wrapping her sleek body around the pole was no feat for Sacha Devine. She was a professional dance instructor. However, hanging upside down and making her ass clap to the beat of the music was a great challenge.

The audience liked it and encouraged Sacha with applause and money. It was not long before blood rushed to her head sending her spiraling down the pole with her legs spread wide open giving the men and women in the club a nice view of her fat cat.

When she finally made it to ground zero she had to get on all fours to regain her composure. She noticed her fiancé and his friend waving for her to come to them. He told her that he did not know she was dancing again. She played the role to see how far the conversation would go.

Left out of the conversation, Ky'am's friend introduced herself as Casey. She had no clue that real Sacha was Kyam's future sister in law. She rubbed her boobs together licking them one at a time. Casey asked her to give her a lap dance when the set was over.

Sacha could not have planned her revenge better. When she finished her set she gave Casey the ultimate lap dance. She straddled Casey's lap with her back facing her. Sacha bounced up and down touching Casey's breasts with her ass making Casey's nipples erect. She even let Casey tickle her ass with her soft hands as she gyrated to the beat of "Africa Bambata."

When Sacha turned to face Casey with her bikini top down she gave Casey an up close and personal view of her very perky breasts. Casey pulled Sacha down closer to her mouth and very directly asked Sacha for a private dance. She hesitated to give an answer at first, but then realized that a private dance would give her the opportunity to give Ky'am the payback he would never forget.

As Sacha led them to the very plush and secluded VIP room she felt her stomach knot up. She was not sure what was going to take place in the room or how she would feel when it was over. Before she could get the door secured they were both seated. Sacha took a seat between the two of them. Since it was Casey's idea for the private dance she asked her, and not Ky'am, what it was that she wanted to see her do that she could not do on the stage. Casey answered by sticking her tongue down Sacha's throat.

Sacha was uncomfortable but she went with the flow. Ky'am had a look on his face that gave Sacha the impression that he was not sure whether he could participate. It was obvious that he was apprehensive because he was not sure if Sacha would divulge his behavior to her identical twin. Sacha decided to reveal that she was Niima and not Nidra.

Instead of telling him I simply removed my G-string exposing to him his name tattooed on my clean-shaven crotch. Ky'am realized that I was his fiancé and not his soon to be sister-in-law. His mouth hung open.

I snickered at him asking, "Does the cat or Sacha have your tongue"? Casey continued to rub on my back, as she was informed of my relationship to Ky'am. She did not seem bothered by the fact that I was his fiancé and not Sacha Devine, the exotic dancer. In fact she wanted him to physically participate in our private dance.

I was against Ky'am doing any thing other than watching. I told him that he was going to regret lying to me and coming here with Casey and that he'd wish that he accompanied me as I requested.

I acted in rare form and experienced my first sexual encounter with the same sex. Since I was the rookie in the situation I laid on the stiff, warm leather couch relinquishing all control to Casey, the expert. After tenderly kissing my body from top to bottom she played with my pussy with her long tongue. Ky'am jacked his dick and looked on with pleasure. He seemed satisfied being able to watch what he, instead of Casey should have been giving me.

My clit never felt better and I was a bit ashamed that I found gratification from a woman touching me sexually. All that changed suddenly when Casey found my G-spot with her fingers and caused an eruption of fluid. This was something no man had ever accomplished. It was feeling good but I drew the line when Casey asked me to reciprocate.

She did not push but asked if we could keep in touch. Just to push Ky'am's buttons I took Casey's number. Before I left the room I gave all the tips that I made that evening to Ky'am. Whispering in his ear that he should not have lied to me I urged him to take the money because he was going to needed it to find him new a place to live.

What's done in the Dark Will Be Caught on Tape?

01-11-02

Dear Confessional:

I am writing you because if I reveal this information to anyone else my life will be in jeopardy. The last time I wrote you I told you that I had a very strong feeling that my boyfriend, Julian, of two years is seeing someone other than me. It was very imperative that I find out for sure. My health, as well as my feelings, are at risk. Julian and I started having unprotected sex after dating for over a year. Yeah, I know what you are thinking, but we agreed that our relationship would be monogamous. Besides, we went together and got tested.

The relationship had being going smooth until our hot and steamy love life had come to an irritating yield. We went from having sex five days a week to maybe once a month. This was conspicuous to me because, Julian's appetite for my juices was insatiable—at least, so I thought. Before I could confront Julian with what I was thinking a woman named Monica called me. She revealed to me that she and Julian had been heavily involved after knowing each other for only a month. She claimed that they never wore condoms and wanted to know if Julian and I did. After talking for an hour I thanked the caller for the 411.

Of course I confronted Julian with what I was told and he simply denied it. He said Monica was a woman from his past. He claimed that she was scorned from their breakup five years ago and would go to any length to make his life a living hell.

Well, although I knew in my heart that Julian was lying, I continued to go out with him. I planned to get hardcore evidence that Julian could not lie about. Our relationship never returned to the way it once was because I refused to sleep with Julian without protection. I would not suck his dick.

Julian was sex crazed. Although we were not intimate I knew he was getting his rocks off somewhere. To confirm my suspicions I placed a voice-activated, audio/visual recorder on a shelf in his bedroom. I was not concerned about Julian finding the device because he gave me the shelf for my belongings that I left in his apartment. The recorder had thirty hours worth of recording time on the hard drive. This gave Julian plenty of time to hang himself.

When I retrieved the recorder from Julian's it reminded me of show and tell. Julian had slept with woman after woman in four days— sometimes three in one day. None of that was as shocking as what I learned after that!

I was about to turn off the TV, when I was pushed down by the shock of the two figures that appeared on the screen.

My mind was blown as I watched Julian get his dick sucked and then become penetrated by his roommate, Terrance. Julian was on the fucking down low! No wonder he was always trying to get me to have anal sex with him. EWWWWW!

I have been tested for HIV every six months for the past two years with no signs of the virus. I am disturbed to say that I have recently been informed by Julian, that he is HIV positive. Out of anger Julian revealed to me that despite the monster running through his body he continues to sleep, unprotected, with innocent women (and probably men). He does this without caring for the lives and/or families he is destroying. I want to tell someone but I am in fear for my life. Julian threatened to kill me if I told anyone his secret.

Enter.Cum

09-24-05

Dear Confessional:

Sweat dropped in my eye as I admired the ladies whose tight gym clothes enhanced their physiques. Normally I would not give the women in the gym a second glance. Right now my wife was in the fifth month of her six-month tour of the Caribbean promoting her latest record. This is the longest we have been apart since we got married seven years ago. I usually join her on her tours but this time someone had to stay home with our bundle of joy, Zana.

Naturally I was missing Jordan, and although everything on the home front is well and good I can't control my sexual impulses. Jordan's long absence has left me lacking in the sex department. Not getting any sexual attention is very hard to adjust to. I'm used to getting' it on the regular.

With one more month before Jordan is to
return home, I could no longer ignore my
appetite for Jordan's lovin'. I had to invent a
way to satisfy my sexual yearnings for my
wife. I was not very fond of masturbation
unless Jordan was around to watch. Now I
was not sure of how to diffuse my urges.

I would not dare cheat on my wife, I have
been around the block a couple of times and I
am wise enough to know that there is no one
out there worth risking my family for. With
nothing else to do when I got home from the
gym I decided to do some web designs for my
clients. I could work before the nanny brought
the baby home. Work always took my mind
off of my troubles.

When my work thinned out my impulses
began to frustrate me again. I decided to visit
an online site that one of my clients started. He
boasted that Enter.Cum was a hands-off,
harmless but pleasurable outlet for men and
women in need of sexual release. Hey, it was a
start.

I registered on the site as D-Rex and found
that Enter.Cum did not leave much to the
imagination. There were all kinds of people to

engage in a chat with. I initiated a Typesation with KissWet. She was intriguing and stimulating which led us into an hour-long computer meeting about everything except sex. I began to feel guilty for what I was doing and gave KissWet a lame excuse for getting off the computer.

But even after the computer experience I went to bed lonely with swollen balls. The next day was the same routine except I could not get KissWet out of my mind. The following day I decided to give Enter.Cum a second chance. I hoped that KissWet had the same idea.

After fighting with my computer I logged on to the Website. I was smiling when I discovered that KissWet was already online. Just as the night before, I started the conversation between the two of us. I was elated that she would talk to me after the way I ended our session the night before.

"Hi there D-Rex. I was not expecting to see your name on my computer screen again after your abrupt departure last night."

"Yeah, well I couldn't stop thinking about you."

"And what were you thinking about big boy?"

"Wouldn't you like to know? No, really, I couldn't stop wondering how you came up with the name KissWet."

"That's easy. Every time someone kisses my jewel I get wet. Since we're on names, where does D-Rex come from?

"The name speaks for itself really—I mean D is my dick and Rex, like a dinosaur, is indicative of it's massiveness."

"Now that we are comfortable enough to talk about sex why don't we engage in a little cyber sex?"

"You don't waste any time, do you KissWet? You must do this on a regular basis."

"Actually...last night was the first time I had ever been on the site. I only signed on out of boredom."

"That's funny because last night was my first time on Enter.Cum too. I must admit that I visited out of more than just boredom. I was, and still am, looking for some action."

"Well let the games begin, D-Rex!"
What have I gotten myself into? Well, here goes nothing.

Not sure of KissWet's likes and dislikes I began touching her softly with my keystrokes.

"KissWet, tell me how you want it."

"I want to rub you with my lips, wetting your tickler so that he will slide deep inside me. Do you like the way I massage your scrotum with my tongue?"

"Yes it feels so good, but can you put both of them in your mouth at the same time? I would really love it if you would."

"Anything for you D-Rex, but first let me lick your swollenness from its tip down to your balls."

"Stop it. You are going to make me explode! Man...you feel good!"

"Ok. I'll just ease your head down my breasts past my navel and right into my treasure chest. Please be careful with my jewel, she is very precious to me."

"Don't worry sexy, I'm just going to take her in and out of my mouth with my tongue while I fondle your insides with my middle finger."

"Deeper D-Rex, deeper."

"Oh, I like it when you type my name, do it again."

"D-Rex, D-Rex, D-Rex, stick your tongue in my pleasure chest...NOW."

"Aren't we a little demanding? Say please and I'll stick it all the way in."

"PLEASE...fuck me with your tongue, D-Rex."

"Only if you let me kiss your spice island afterwards."

"ANYTHING!"

"Now I know exactly why you call yourself KissWet. I almost needed a lifeguard to save me from drowning in your juices."

"I told you. Now tell me—what do I have to do to make your liquid flow?"

"A lot, but first I wanna watch you spread your treasure chest open while I stroke my jack-in- the-box."

"Is it wide enough for you? Can you see the hidden treasure?"

"Yes—and I can't wait to feel it with my instrument. Keep caressing her while I get my biological response ready to go to work on her."

"Ok—but I gotta warn you, if I keep touching myself I'm going to explode."

"Hold on a minute, little lady. I want us to cum together. I'm ready to stick my big friend inside of your wetness. Are you ready to feel D-Rex, Baby?"

"I'm so, so ready for D-Rex to eat me up."

"Before I put him in I want you to promise that when we get ready to cum we both press 'enter' on our keyboards. That way we can watch one another climax. Deal?"

"Deal."

"Oh my gosh, KissWet, you're wet and warm on the inside. Keep gyrating on me and I'm going to let go all over your pleasure chest."

"I'm going to gyrate baby, 'cause I'm ready to cum all over your dick."

"Fine, I'm ready to cum too. Don't forget to push enter so we can see one another through our webcams."

"Ready, set, ENTER!"

I got the orgasm of my life, and what was more exciting was realizing that the woman I had been having cyber sex with was none other than my beautiful wife, Jordan! What an orgasmic surprise! I guess she must have been longing for me as much as I was her.

We, Myself, and My Pussy

5-24-04

My Dear Confessional:

It is hard to find a man who has a complete package. I've found that in each man there is one maybe two assets that I like. For example one guy may be very intellectual but horrible in bed. Or another man can be the master under the sheets, but can't hold a job. Like I said it is hard to find everything in one man that I require.

We, myself, and my pussy would love to
have a man who is well hung—
with KNOWLEDGE
COMPASSION and SPIRTUALITY
this is the access key
allowing him to penetrate me, us, we mentally,
emotionally, and of course, physically.

My heart desires a man who is always erect for
me—standing tall by my side

wholeheartedly with his soul and mind
backing me through thick and thin,
with his support there is no challenge, big or
small, we cannot win.

I want a man who is not afraid to cum—
to me in his time of need
confiding in me when his heart bleeds
allowing me to be his pillow as he is my rock,
reassurance that he will always be on top.

We myself and my pussy demand
a man who can stroke us good
caressing us with words
stimulating our physique with love,
with the tip of his tongue he can take us to the
ultimate peak,
making love to our mind,
before he loves us from behind,
making each moment spent with him worth
the time.

Wife Keeper

7-02-06

Confessional:

My guilty conscience is the only thing The Clean-Up Man could not tidy up for me. Come to think of it he was cleaning when we met. I was at the post office waiting in line to mail an oversized package when The Clean-Up Man, who I now sometimes call CUM for short, overheard me talking to my girlfriend on my cell phone. I imagine I must have been a bit loud because I later learned that he heard my entire conversation.

He got my attention by introducing himself and then giving me his business card. He owned a janitorial service and wanted to offer his services, for payment of course, after all he heard me complaining to Fenise about my messy home, that I had no time to clean.

Although I desperately needed someone to keep house I knew with out a doubt that Cody, my husband, would never approve of a well-kept, attractive, male domestic engineer in his home, with his wife. After contemplating the idea for months I finally decided to give The Clean-Up Man a call.

Between work, teaching, and his social life I rarely saw my husband. I could have two clean up men and he would never know because he is never home. I arranged for The Clean-Up Man to come over when I was sure my husband was out of town on business, which was the same time every week. The routine went on for months with out any problems. The Clean-Up Man cleaned house and I worked out of my office, a loft over my garage.

For some reason I began to feel lonely for companionship. My girlfriends and other social circles didn't seem to occupy my time like they once did. I realized that I was yearning for my husbands company. I missed our in depth conversations, long walks, dinner on the beach and most importantly intimacy. Yes, we had sex every so often. But Cody was to often pressed for time, which meant, when ever we did have sex it was quick and to the point.

The Clean-Up Man was the only man that I came in contact with on a regular basis. At night when my hormones began calling my name I found myself fantasizing about my housekeeper. I would lie in bed imagining his tongue suckling my breast as I massaged my Kitty. I tried to force his image out of my mind, but no matter how much I tried, I could not get his face out of my mind.

As time went by, I wondered more and more what it would be like to be with The Clean-Up Man. Not just in bed, but I was curious as to what he would be like as a loving husband, that had time for his wife. Frustrated with my situation and an undersexed libido I decided to do something and stop suffering in silence.

Instead of retreating to the garage when The Clean-Up Man arrived at my home I stayed in the house. I tried to make small talk with him, but he always seemed preoccupied in his own thoughts. I followed him from room to room, but he still would not pay me any attention. I felt stupid and backed off for a week or two.

When I finally built my courage back up to approach The Clean-Up Man again, I had a fail proof plan that guaranteed to get me what I wanted. CUM stood at my door in shock when he entered the living room and all I had on was a Chiffon robe exposing my satin thongs, bustier and garter belt. I followed him from the living room to the dinning to the great room as he tried to find something to clean in my already immaculate home. With each room he went into I removed a piece of clothing showing more and more skin. Each time The Clean-Up Man looked at me I could see the hunger in his eyes. It was when I took off my right heel, the last thing on my body, that I knew I had CUM where I wanted him—erect and salivating to feel my warmth.

At first the ceramic tile on the Kitchen floor was cold, but warmed up soon after The Clean-Up Man and I rolled around on it, making it our very heated oversized love nest. Despite our extracurricular activities the house was so quiet you could hear a pen drop. That did not last long after CUM took whip cream out of the fridge and spread it all over my pussy with his aggressive tongue. My screams of delight could be heard a mile away, he fucked my pussy so good with his oral treasure. I could not get my knees to stop shaking from the way he nibbled on my clit. I'm assuming he thought I could not handle him wetting my pussy with his mouth. Suddenly he stopped and when I sat up to see why he suspended his tongue strokes. He guided my head gently towards his dick, which I gleefully sucked and sucked, licked and fondled his dick, while blowing on his happy sacks. My patience grew thin and I could not wait any longer to feel him inside of me. The foreplay was great, I mean my toes were definitely curled, but I was ready to fell an object inside of me. At the peak of the day only The Clean-Up Man's dick would suffice.

Both lying on our sides I guided his dick into my Pussy. He was so large that it took some time getting his member all the way inside. Once our parts connected, it was hard for us to part. We only stopped to lubricate every so often. I think we fucked all over the kitchen, including on top of my brand new cook top. The Clean-Up Man ejaculated all over my legs—before I had the chance to cum a second time.

To my amazement he did not leave me disappointed. CUM thrust me back on the island, while he tickled my prawn with his wonder tongue all the while sticking his middle finger in and out of my wetness creating enough tension for me to climax once more.

After our first encounter together it was impossible for The Clean-Up Man and I not to indulge in each other a second time, which of course, led to a regular routine. Yes. Cum is a wife keeper now, and he does such a good job at it that I had to hire another cleaning service to clean my home. I want The Clean-Up Man to put all of his energy on keeping me satisfied.

Somebody Else Will

1-2-05

Dear Confessional:

Imagine a mother doing the tango with her daughter's boyfriend. Well I know how it sounds but Amber brought it on herself. Always calling me bragging on how good Anthony is in bed.

"Hello mother how are you?"

"I'm fine Amber. What do I owe the honor of this call?"

"Uh, Uh, Uh! Mom you would not believe how Anthony puts it down in bed. I mean, the dick is sooo good and when he goes down south my knees buckle. Until Anthony I never knew what it was like for a man to put his mouth down there. I tell you Anthony has laid all my uncertainties about oral copulation to sleep."

"Don't let it go to your head now Amber, he just might want you to return the favor. We both know you are too prissy to get your knees dirty, besides you probably can't put his dick in your mouth without gagging."

"Mom you are disgusting, and no I don't get down like that. Anthony could lick me from my rudda all the way to my todda and I still won't consider giving him a blow job."

"That's selfish Amber, and I did not teach you to be that way, I taught you to share. As they 'say one good turn deserves another.' Besides, do you really think that Anthony is going to keep pleasing you and you not reciprocate? I am going to tell you like someone once told me, if you don't someone else will."

"Mom, please stop it, Anthony is not going anywhere, and I do things to compensate for the things I fall short on."

"Yea okay, but don't say I did not warn you. You gotta keep your man happy. Since clearly you didn't call me for advice, why don't you finish telling me how Anthony keeps your nose wide open?"

"Girl just where should I begin? Last night he insisted that I come over his house with my full length Mink coat on. When I got there he directed me to his favorite chair where he spreads my legs and lifted them over his broad shoulders and sops me up like wet biscuits and gravy. After he wets me up like Niagara Falls he slides right in my pussy with his 10inches of…"

"Amber I've heard enough! I don't know whether to be ashamed or turned on by all the details you have shared."

"You said to finish telling you how Anthony keeps my nose open."

"I know, I know, I asked more than I bargained for, and I am sorry. If you don't mind I am going to go dream about getting my pussy tampered with. Call me tomorrow so I can tell you how it went."

"Mom you don't have to have dreams. Go out with one of those men that keep chasing you around. I bet they can get you wet."

"Bye Amber!"

Somebody Else Will II

1-3-05

Dear Confessional:

My girls' mother has been chasing me down relentlessly the past week. If I didn't know any better I would think she thought that I was her man and not her daughters. Well I won't be Amber's man for long if she finds out what happened between me and her mother. Ms. Greye forced herself on me, but that's not an excuse because I shoulda been stronger. Damn though I couldn't resist Ms. Greye.

Yesterday Ms. Greye called me complaining about some clogged plumbing so I went over with my tools after work. I though it was strange that Ms. Greye opened the door with a robe and makeup on. Apprehensively, I followed her to the bathroom where she was having problems. She left saying she would be in her room and if I needed her to give her a holla.

Thirty minutes went by and I was lying on my back inside the vanity replacing the old pipes with new ones. When I slid from under the sink I was faced with Ms. Greye's gray pussy eyeing me. I was taken aback. I attempted to get up, when Ms. Greye and her naked pussy jumped on my face. I absolutely forgot about my relationship to Ms. Greyes daughter. I grabbed her and greedily stuck my tongue in and out of her seasoned crotch. Just as I was getting into it Ms. Greye stopped me. I was not expecting Ms. Greye to unzip my pants with her teeth but she did. Once she got my manhood loose she preceded to tea bag my nuts before she put my dick in her tight mouth.

Sitting on the toilet as I stood in front of her Ms. Greye made me feel good. It had been a long time since I had my jack in the box released by a damp, warm mouth. Ms. Greye wouldn't let go of my dick until she saw the white stuff seep from it. I climaxed so hard I was dizzy. Ms. Greye is the original "Superhead". *I never had a lube job like that before,* I thought to myself as I wiped the perspiration from my forehead.

For some reason Ms. Greye felt the need to tell me that there was no need for me to feel guilty because of what happened between us.

She told me that she was aware that I was not getting any head action at home. With a smile on her face Ms. Greye said that she was doing both Amber and me a favor by keeping it in the family.

I drove to Amber's with a smile on my face. The first thing Amber noticed was the lipstick on my cheek; I told her that her mother kissed me for fixing her clogged plumbing.

Expression

2-03-30

Dear Confessional:

   Because I find it difficult to talk nasty to my husband, I wrote him a poem to express my kinkiness to him and here it goes.

Coming at you with some spontaneous shit,
shit that make you ask yourself
what is wrong with this chick.

As you enter the door from a long days work
 I greet you naked with a smirk
And—of course, a juicy wet kiss.

It's time for you to put in your overtime,
 make love to me quick!
I miss you and you know that you have been
running naked through my dirty mind.

Just the mere thought of you makes me feel
freaky inside

nothing feels better than when you
Kiss me,
lick me,
fuck me,
please me.

No! I cannot wait and give you a chance to chill
I am ready for your big dick.
You know—the one you call thrill!

Just lie down,
give me what I want
you inside of me
taking me to the heavens and back to earth
give it a chance I'll show you what it's worth.

Epilogue

Wiping the sweat from his forehead with the back of his hand, the committee president asks Simone to leave the room while he and the board review her project. In the very next room Simone is replaying her performance in the boardroom. Her thoughts are broken by loud moans, grunts and the sound of skin slapping in the boardroom. Simone begins to smile as she realizes that her project was a success.

If I can get the board aroused with my patients' confessions the way I get stimulated, that PhD is just signatures away from being mine.

After hours of pure, unadulterated sex the board members leave the room one by one, making Simone's heart sink.

This cannot be a good sign. If I were going to be granted my Doctorate all the committee members should be present to give me the decision.

Simone's fears were laid to rest as the president of the committee invited her back into the boardroom.

"Miss Simone Cox please have a seat. I know you are probably wondering why the other

members have left the room. I can assure you
it is in your best interest that we be alone. I
will start by telling you that after much
consideration the board and I have decided to
grant you your Doctorate in Psychology."

Simone's face began to widen. Her lips and
eyes were smiling at her accomplishment.
Simone is so lost in her own thoughts that she
almost does not hear the president as he gives
her his second reason for wanting the two of
them alone in the boardroom.

"Simone I am happy to be the only one to
present you with this degree. I feel inclined to
add a little more than I would for any other
doctoral candidate. I could tell from the way
you read your patients confessions seductively,
using your hands to touch yourself from time
to time, and the way you moistened your
lips...that you have been lacking a man's
touch. In addition to your degree today I
would like to give you something extra, that is,
if you don't mind."

Simone spread her legs open signaling to the
president that she welcomed his touch. When
the president saw the string caught in between
Simone's pussy lips, he didn't waste any time.

He unzipped his slacks and released his pet from his pants so that he could put it in Simone's cage.

The president stroked himself as Simone played with herself, sticking multiple fingers in and out of her pussy. She and the president teased one another like this for minutes, each waiting for the other to make the first move. The president gave in bending Simone over a high back chair, hiking her skirt up and pulling Simon's La Perla G-String over so that he could lick her chocolate speedway. Simone helped him out by spreading her cheeks giving him full access to her backside. The rim job sent sparks through Simone, making her do something she never did during sex...talk nasty.

Simone's level of participation turned the president on more as he stuck his fingers into her moist hole causing her to buck and grind all over his face. When Simone was wet to his satisfaction he got off of his knees leaving his fingers in her pussy and used them to guide his dick into her womanhood. First, giving Simone slow but filling strokes as he increased the pace. Simone's moans became louder.

Simone liked the way he gave it to her so roughly. She, in turn, gave him everything she possessed. Their tryst lasted through the rest of the day into the rest of their lives.

Simone was happy and relieved to receive her degree. Finally, she could lead a normal life again without studying and research. She freed herself up, which allowed her to engage in her own sexual escapades and still treat her patients with theirs.

About the Author

Fauzykiss is a proud mother of one and works as a dental assistant. She is currently working toward a degree in Africana Studies/Psychology at Wayne State University.

Fauzykiss writes as a means of expression. In her spare time she enjoys cooking and painting. To escape everyday stress she reads erotica, suspense, and urban fiction. She also finds sharing her stories with family and friends entertaining and self-fulfilling. Her stories are inspired by contemporary life in a large urban city.

Fauzykiss is a native of Detroit, Michigan where she proudly resides with her loved ones and is hard at work on her sophomore novel *Urban Avenge.*

Erogenous Confessions

Coming Soon….

Urban
Avenger
An
Urban Suspense

Erogenous Confessions
ORDER FORM
P.O. BOX 19460 · Detroit, MI 48219
www.fauzykiss.com

Customer Information

Name:	
Address:	
City:	
State / Zip:	

Purchase Information

Erogenous Confessions	$14.95
No. of Copies	**X**___
Sub Total:	
Sales Tax (6% MI)	$___
Shipping & Handling (USPS)	$3.95
GRAND TOTAL:	$___

Shipping Information
(If Address Different than Above)

Name:	
Address:	
City:	
State / Zip:	

Autographed Copy to say:

ATTENTION:

Calling All Aspiring Authors!!!!

Short Erotic Story Contest

Cash Prize $50.00 and story will be printed in Fauzykiss' next book.

Mail entries to:
Fauzykiss
Short Story Contest
P.O. Box 19460
Detroit, Michigan 48219

Please send all stories typed or printed on 8 ½ x 11 sized paper. Include name, address, phone number and self addressed stamped envelope (SASE) for consideration.

Entries will not be returned to contestants and will be destroyed to protect the writer and the content. Erotic story lines with children or violent rape scenes will not be considered and will be destroyed with no liability to the reader or publisher. The winning material will retain all rights and privileges as the original writer of the winning material.